T0368911

The Chase 2

MARILYN MITCHELL STATON

iUniverse®

THE CHASE 2

iUniverse books may be ordered through booksellers or by contacting:

iUniverse
1663 Liberty Drive
Bloomington, IN 47403
www.iuniverse.com
1-800-Authors (1-800-288-4677)

ISBN: 978-1-5320-7728-9 (sc)
ISBN: 978-1-5320-7729-6 (e)

Print information available on the last page.

iUniverse rev. date: 01/25/2020

Dillon and I returned to my apartment after the wedding disaster. We both were so incredibly happy about how things had turned out for us. As soon as we entered my apartment, we held each other so close and tight, not wanting to let go.

After holding each other, Dillon began to look around at my place. He was in awe. Finally he said, "Ruby, this is really a nice place. You have to make a lot of money to afford something like this. Ruby, are you rich?"

I looked at him and laughed. "No, silly, but I do very well with my practice."

We sat down and talked for hours into the night. We discussed our plans for the future.

Dillon said, "Ruby, I really meant it when I asked you to marry me at the church. You're the first and only woman I've ever felt this way about. So I'm asking you again, Ruby." This time he was on bended knees. Dillon proposed to me very sincerely with a slight tear in his eyes and a gulp in his speech. "Please, Ruby, will you marry me?"

My heart leaped with joy. I was so overwhelmed with the love I felt for this man at the moment that tears streamed down my cheeks. I was speechless, although I knew this moment was coming. I just didn't know how or when. The way he expressed himself was so beautiful.

I wasn't responding quickly enough, so he continued to say, "You are my queen, a woman to be adored and admired into eternity. There's none other like you. You hold the key to my heart. My heart is locked down only for you."

At that point, the only response to that had to be, "Yes, Dillon, I will marry you." It was if my knight in shining armor had kneeled down before me. His submissive manner humbled me, but yet he was in control in every way. I too kneeled down as I gave my answer. "Yes, Sir Dillon Dalton, I will marry you. You too are my king that I would always love, cherish, and honor forever."

Dillon was all man in every way. He could be strong when need be, along with compassionate and understanding. I think at this moment I had seen every side of Dillon.

We committed ourselves to each another that night without an official wedding ceremony, which was to come later. We were both exhausted from the day, so we decided to turn in for the night.

Dillon, being himself of course, tried to persuade me into sleeping with him that night, but he backed off when I reminded him of what I stood for (no sex before marriage). And of course he reminded me that we had already "been there done that." I had to stand my ground and be strong.

"Could I just hold you in his arms as we slept?" he asked.

"Yes, and that's it. No funny stuff."

Then I had to ask myself, *Why did I agree to do that?* I knew how great the temptation would be. I tried to be strong of course, but as I lay there in his arms, it felt as if my body were melting into his with so much desire.

So I pushed him away. "You will have to sleep in the other bedroom."

The next day when I got up, Dillon had made breakfast, which was pretty delicious.

Dillon proceeded to talk about the land that he and his brothers had just split. "I want you to ride back with me to Kentucky to take a look at it."

I agreed to go with him because I had taken time off work due to the original wedding with Bryan. I packed a few things and called my friend, Katherine, to let her know that I was going with Dillon to Kentucky for a few days and that I loved her and appreciated everything she had done in helping me prepare for the wedding.

Katherine asked, "Are you sure that's what you want to do, considering all that you've been through." She then paused for a moment. "Are you and Dillon going to elope?"

"Of course not. Don't worry. I will let you know when the wedding will take place." I could feel the expression on her face over the phone. That was just how well I knew Katherine.

She nodded with a big grin on her face. "You better."

Dillon and I left early in the morning. We decided to drive my car. The drive once again was breathtaking. The mountain's landscape was magnificent, stretching across the blue sky as though it was the gateway to heaven. It looked as though if we stood on the mountaintops, we could just walk right into heaven's doors.

Looking down was another spectacular beauty. In the meadows and valleys, when feasting our eyes upon these natural wonders, there were begonias, angelonias, and sneeze weeds, just to name a few. For a few moments, one could forget all their troubles and worries that threatened them. Dillon was accustomed to the scenery, because he had lived there all his life, so I don't think he quite saw it the way I did.

Dillon and I had gotten almost to his home when we decided to stop at a convenience store for gas. We both went inside and got snacks. Upon leaving, we met Jasper and Roscoe coming in. They looked at us with disgust written all over their faces.

They came out while Dillon was pumping gas and looked over at my car, a 2018 Camara SS 6.2. They were driving an older car that looked as though it had been remodeled, maybe a 1971 Chevy SS with a 454 engine, nickname "Heavy Chevy."

After looking back at it once more, I was sure that's what it was. It was pretty well put together for an older car. It had a black exterior with red seats, a spoiler on the hood, and nice tires and rims. It ran like a hummingbird. I was also a car fanatic. I couldn't help it. I liked old and new cars.

I told Dillon as he was pumping the gas, "When I was younger, my friends and I would sneak to car shows. We would sometimes even sneak away from home, gather at a deserted area, and race each other until dawn. Not only did the guys race, but the girls did too. We were not afraid."

Roscoe and Jasper got into their car and watched us as though they were waiting for something. They pulled up their car right beside ours. The first thought that crossed my mind was that they wanted to start something again, like another fight.

But this time I was ready. I braced myself for the worst. I was not going to sit by and just let them beat Dillon. My heart was beating fast, and my palms were sweating. I had a .357 Magnum under the seat, but Dillon didn't know it. I know. Some Christian, huh? Oh yes, I was taught to live and die by the sword, although we know that's not how the scripture is really quoted.

Dillon was staring back at them with a stern look on his face as well. I could tell he was ready for whatever they wanted to do. Jasper looked over at us. He was on the passenger side.

He said, "Come on, Dillon. Let's do it."

Dillon asked, "Do what?" Dillon looked at me and I at him. Dillon said, "These guys know I don't race, and it's all because of what I'm driving. All I've ever raced is a horse." He had a puzzled look on his face. "Ruby, I'm not about to do this to your car. No way."

I looked at the road in front of us, a straight shot with no trees on either side of the road or traffic. Apparently Roscoe and Jasper had raced this stretch before because it was a perfect place.

I told Dillon, "If you don't, I will."

He looked at me. "What? Oh no you won't!"

"Look, Dillon," I explained. "I know this car. We can beat them. I made a few changes to my engine just for moments like this because I figure if you're gonna buy a sports car, then that car should live up to its name."

By that time, Jasper yelled over, "What's it gonna be? Oh, I see that pretty little sissy car doesn't have any power, huh!"

Well, that figures, I thought. Okay, that was just too much. I couldn't take it anymore. I told Dillon, "Let's switch over. I'll drive."

Dillon kept saying, "Stop, Ruby. You can't know what you're doing. These guys have been racing and building cars all their lives."

"I may not build them, but I sure can drive them."

We switched over, and Jasper yelled, "Come on! A girl gonna drive the little sissy car and beat us! You got to be kidding me!"

I glimpsed over at Roscoe, who was driving their car. He shook his head, as in disbelief.

"Buckle up, Dillon. I love and respect you, but sometimes a girl gotta do what a girl gotta do. It's time to kick butt."

Dillon looked at me as if I had lost my mind. At that moment, he might have thought right because in those few moments, my thoughts went back to when I was a teenager and feeling the thrill of a race. These were the two goons who had insulted us at the barn dance, and this was how I would get my revenge. I was so gung-ho that I didn't even allow the Word of God to penetrate my thoughts. "Vengence is mine, saith the Lord. I will repay." Little did they know what my car was capable of. Dillon had begun to sweat and look a little nervous, but I wasn't sweating. It wasn't a man's job.

I told Jasper, "Shut up and let's do it!"

"Okay," he said in a sarcastic manner. "Little girl in big-girl panties, come on. I'm going to knock on my car door three times, and on the third knock, let's do it."

Roscoe was revving up his engine as Jasper counted. On the third knock, we jetted off together. Jasper was slightly in front of me. I allowed him to get in front of me about three car lengths. Knowing the power my car had, I was not intimidated the least.

Dillon was crossing his chest with his hands as to make a cross and praying. The Chevy now was well ahead of me as though they were winning, but not so. I pressed on my gas pedal, slowly increasing my speed to catch up with them, and when I did, they pressed on harder to pass but couldn't.

We were now side by side. I pressed on the accelerator, and I could feel the back end of my car drop a little as it gained more speed. My Camaro felt as though it was hugging the road as it passed the Chevy, almost like doing a walk by. So I shot by the Chevy like a bolt of lightning. I knew I had won. I slowed down and came to a stop. The Chevy went on as they slowed down, knowing they had lost. They were too embarrassed to stop.

Dillon hopped out of the car and kissed the ground. Then he came around to the driver's side and demanded I get out. He grabbed the keys out of my hand. "I thought I knew you, Ruby, but apparently I don't." He spoke in an angry tone, hitting the steering wheel.

"Hey, look, Dillon! We won! I thought you would be happy. Come on."

"But at what expense, Ruby, that we both die, and where did you learn to drive like that?"

"Haven't you been listening to me, Dillon? Remember—I told you that I used to race cars with my friends when we were teenagers."

"Wow, so much for growing up in a Christian home, huh?"

"Just because your parents are Christians doesn't mean the children are. That is a misconception that so many people have. Just remember, Dillon, that parents can teach their children the right way to go, but that doesn't mean the child will always make the right choices, especially when they come of age. Also, Dillon, as a Christian person, you are not perfect. There are things you have to learn and grow, thereby taking one step and one day at a time."

He looked at me. "Ruby, do you think what you just did was right in the sight of God?"

"Of course not, Dillon. I know racing is against the law on a public highway. Okay, I went over and beyond the law. That's another thing I must repent of."

He began to calm down.

I looked at him. "Dillon, wasn't it fun though? Couldn't you just feel that adrenaline flowing through your body like a rush?"

Dillon said with a slight grin on his face, "Yea, like a rush to get out of your car. You are one complicated woman. When I think I've got you figured out, you flip on me. You're always doing something new that just boggles my mind, Ruby. Although I do find that a little interesting about you. You are definitely not a boring lady. That's for sure."

"Oh no! You can't say a word. Look at what you did."

He had a puzzled look etched across his face. "What? What did I do?"

"Come on, Dillon! Busting up a wedding! What would you call that?"

"I would call that coming to get what's mine." And then he proceeded to laugh in a subtle manner.

After the race, Dillon and I found a nearby motel for the night. The next day we headed out to look over the land. It was quite a beautiful spring day with only a few clouds in the big blue sky. The wind was slightly blowing with a warm breeze. We could hear the birds chirping as though they were making music, each making a different sound yet simultaneously in rhythm with another. The earth seemed as though it had just come alive, bursting with life everywhere we looked.

While approaching the area of land, Dillon said, "Let's start on the west side and work our way back east. Maybe if we go that way, we won't run into Clyde and Rusty. I don't want them to know you're here with me right now. They will only start trouble for us. I don't want you to have to go through any of what you went through before."

I was thinking the same thing, and I didn't want to either.

Dillon continued, "I'll tell them about us later."

I agreed with him. So we did exactly what Dillon had planned. The land that was given to Dillon was very nice. Some parts were not so great, but overall it was beautiful.

Afterward Dillon and I were coming around a curve on the road, and as we were coming out of the curve, we passed a truck.

Dillon said, "Oh no! That was them, but I don't think they recognized us because you've changed cars since you left. I'm just not in the mood for them today." He began to go a little faster.

"Why did you speed up?"

"I want to get you out of the area as quickly as possible."

"Please slow down."

Dillon looked over at me. "Oh, you're a fine one to talk Ms. Race Car Driver." He continued to speed.

I was looking at all the trees and the winding curves we were taking. Then all of sudden, Dillon hit something in the road. The car swerved off the road, down into an embankment. We got out of the car. I was a little shaken from the incident, but Dillon seemed to be very calm.

"Are you all right?" He grabbed me and put his arms around me because he noticed that I was a little shaken.

Neither of us were hurt. Dillon tried all he knew to get the car out by backing it and going forward, but it was of no use. The tires were stuck. Now I was getting angry because Dillon should have listened to me. There we were, stuck in the middle of nowhere and no cell phone reception. He continued to try to get the car out, but nothing was working. The harder he tried, the worse it got.

Dillon looked at me with guilt written all over his face. "Well, we will have to climb out of this ditch onto the road."

We got onto the road and walked for about an hour when we heard voices from the woods. Dillon and I looked at one another, puzzled as to what was going on. He grabbed my hand, pulled me off the open road, and put his finger over his lips for me to be quiet. We continued walking, and the voices sounded as though we were getting closer and closer to them.

Dillon and I approached an opening in the woods. He pulled me back a little so they could not see us, and there they were, three men and a woman with their backs turned to us and guns hanging on their side. In front of them was another man down on his knees and blindfolded. One of them had a gun pointed at him.

They were yelling back and forth at each other. I could hear the man on his knees, begging for mercy for them not to kill him. I gasped with astonishment.

9

Dillon put his hand over my mouth. "Shhh."

I couldn't believe what I was seeing. It was too much something like out of a movie, but it was there right in front of me. The man who was pointing the gun at the man on his knees shot him. The poor man fell to the ground.

That was when I fainted, feeling myself slide to the ground. I could faintly hear Dillon telling me, "Wake up. Wake up, Ruby."

He picked me up, throwing his arm around my waist to carry me. That wasn't fast enough so he picked me up in his arms. I began to come around, feeling woozy. Dillon speaking to me in a muffled voice was beginning me to wake up.

"Ruby, they heard us, so we have got to move fast."

I was still feeling weak in my legs, but I gained enough strength in them to stand.

Dillon grabbed my hand. "Come on, Ruby! Run!"

The chase was on. We knew they had guns and we had none. It was no doubt that they intended to do to us what they had just done to that other fellow. Dillon stopped running and looked around.

We were out of breath. All of a sudden, he stretched his arm out across my chest. "Ruby, stop! Look, we have nowhere else to run."

I looked at Dillon, shaking my head. "Sure we do. Just keep on going."

"No, Ruby. Take a closer look. We are surrounded by swampland."

How was I supposed to know? I had never been in a swamp before. We were both now whispering.

"Okay," said Dillon. "This is what we will have to do. We will have to get down in the swamp water and hold our breath."

"Dillon, that's impossible. If we get into that water, there's a chance of getting bit by a snake or anything."

"I know, but I think I'd rather take that chance."

So Dillon started hastily looking around. I didn't know what he was looking for, but he found what he wanted and showed me the sticks in his hand.

"Dillon, we don't have time for games. What is that? What are you going to do with sticks?"

"They're not just sticks. They're reeds. I will break these reeds, and when we slide down in the water, we will hold the reeds in our mouth and hold our noses closed with the other hand."

"No, no, no. There's got to be another way. Just look at that water, Dillon. It's murky with green algae."

By that time, we heard the men getting closer, yelling "Come on out! We just want to talk!"

Dillon put the reed in my hand, and we both slid down into the murky abyss of water. While we lay in the water, we could hear them walking by.

While there, I felt something sliding across my thighs, the very thing that I thought would happen. I wanted to jump up and scream at the top of my voice, but I knew I couldn't, knowing they were there waiting to shoot Dillon and myself. So what did I do? I prayed.

And as I did, I remembered the scripture when Paul accidently picked up a snake. It bit him, and he lived. So I prayed to God while lying in that water that He do with me the same thing He did with Paul in the book of Acts.

When we no longer heard them, Dillon and I began to come up out of the water, and we looked at a horrific sight. We were covered with mud, green algae, and weeds.

Dillon put his finger over his lips. "Shhh!" He pointed to a man standing behind a tree, urinating with his back turned to us.

He zipped his pants and then turned around. He looked at us with his mouth dropped, eyes bulging, and mouth quivering.

He finally got the words to come out. "What the hell!" He began to reach for his gun.

Dillon was faster. He grabbed his arm, knocking the man to the ground. The gun fell out of his hands. I started to reach down and grab it, but they were fighting so fiercely that there wasn't a chance. I couldn't get to it without falling back into the water. Dillon was punching him in the face, fighting like a madman.

I told Dillon in a low voice, hoping the others wouldn't hear to stop, "He's had enough."

Dillon finally let him go. The man lay there, barely able to speak, but at least he was alive. Dillon reached down and picked up the gun. "Come on, Ruby. We have to get out of here before they come back looking for this guy." Dillon grabbed me by the hand, and we took off.

I kept looking back to see if he were okay. He was barely moving and groaning at the same time. Although he wanted to kill us, I couldn't see myself killing anyone.

My clothes felt so heavy as we ran with mud all over me from the swamp. The smell of the swamp water was in my nostrils, and the taste was in my mouth, which made me want to gag. I had no idea where Dillon was going, but he knew very well I dared not ask because I knew what he would say. "I know these woods like the back of my hand."

We came upon an old shack in the woods, which could hardly be seen because of all the shrubbery and trees around it.

Dillon said, "Ruby, you will have to stay here while I go and get help because I can move faster if I go by myself."

Oh boy, did I pitch a fit. "Dillon, have you lost your mind? No, no, no way am I going to stay here!"

He held my arms. "Ruby, please. You will be all right. Trust me. No one can see this shack behind all the shrubbery."

Finally I agreed with him. He took off as fast as he could. I went inside, and it was a horrific sight. The walls had been gutted out. The floor creaked as I walked around. It must have been used for hunting a long time ago. There were no windows to look out of. I feared for Dillon as well as for myself. My thoughts were, *What if they catch Dillon?* I knew they would kill him. I just knew they would. My mind was racing back and forth on what if this and that.

And how could Dillon have left me here, and why did I agree to such nonsense? Doubt had riddled my mind as I continued to pace back and forth. But then I heard that little voice say, *Now what is faith? Is it not the substance of things hoped for and the evidence of things not seen?* Yes, then and there, I began to calm down and get a hold of myself. I stopped pacing across the floor for a second because I heard voices outside of the shack. It was them. They had caught up with us.

One of them said, "Well, what is this?"

Another replied, "It looks like an old shack of some kind."

One added, "You know nobody could possibly be in there. The snakes would eat them alive."

Then one said, "There is a sure way to find out. Let's fire a couple of rounds in it. That'll flush 'em out."

Someone stated, "Let's not waste our ammo. Push the bushes out of the way and go in to see what's in there."

It felt as though my heart stopped. I froze as to what to do next. By that time, a big rat ran across my feet. I gasped with almost a scream and caught myself, knowing they were right there. Where the rat ran was a strange place.

There was a gap in the wall, small but yet large enough for me to get through. While they were working hard moving the shrubbery, I pushed some boards back where the opening was and slid through.

After sliding through, I put the boards back in place so they would not see how I got out. To my surprise, I had entered in a tunnel, which offered a peek of light. And oh boy, didn't I thank God for that rat?

I could hear the men in the shack looking around, but I was on my way to freedom. The tunnel led me to the outside. I didn't know where I was, but at least it was daylight and I could see where I was going. I was running quickly and looking back to see if they were behind me, but they weren't.

I turned to look back once more, and that was when I bumped into Floyd, not even looking at him. I just began to scream because I thought it was one of the other men.

Floyd grabbed me by the shoulders. "Ruby! Ruby! It's me, Floyd."

I didn't hear or see him at first. Finally I did look up at him, gasping for breath. I fell on his chest, and I was so relieved that it was him. "I'm so glad to see you." I didn't even ask him what he was doing down there. I was just so happy to see him.

He began to ask me what I was doing down there, but before he could finish, I could hear them coming.

"Floyd, we have to go. We don't have time to talk. There are some really bad guys after me. I will explain later."

We kept running as far as we could, but Floyd, being so overweight, gave out, and that was when they caught up with us. One approached us. It looked as if he might have been the leader. He had a square face, squinted eyes, and black hair hanging over his face.

He looked at Floyd. "Oh, we have a newcomer, huh? What's your name, big fellow?"

Floyd was so out of breath that he couldn't speak. So the man hit Floyd in the stomach as hard as he could with his gun, knocking Floyd to the ground.

He said, "When I ask a question, I expect an answer. Do you hear me? And now say, 'Yes, sir, Mr. Kenny.'"

I tried to help Floyd because I knew he was out of breath. So I spoke up. "His name is Floyd. Can't you see that he is unable to speak right now?"

He looked at me. "Shut up, woman. Speak when you're spoken to. Okay, now we're getting somewhere. So this is Floyd. All right, now we have enough people to have a little party, don't we?" He grinned with a sly smile on his face. "Well, I tell you what we will all do. We will just bunk down right here and wait for that other guy. And what's-his-name, girl, since you're so smart."

"His name is Dillon."

"And what's your name? Since we're all getting acquainted here, my name is Killer. I'm feeling frustrated and tired."

I didn't care at the moment. Kenny grabbed me by the neck with his face in mine. "All right, looks like I've got a wildcat on my hands! I am going to give you another chance. What is your name, girl?"

I finally said, :Ruby."

He then let me go. "Now wasn't that easy? That's a pretty name, almost as pretty as you are. It sounds rich, and I like rich." He then continued, "Yeah, looks like that old boy might be a little sweet on you, so he will definitely be back to get you."

One of the other men said, "Kenny, why don't we just kill 'em and get out of here? How do you know that he won't bring the law back with him?"

"Because I have already checked it out, dummy. They don't have cell phone towers down here, so I doubt if these hillbillies even have a cell phone. The nearest town is about fifty miles away."

He told one of the men to get over there and tie us up and make sure we were tied tight. He tied the rope around my wrist so tight that it felt as if all the blood flow to my hands were shut off.

Kenny turned and looked at the other men, shouting, "I came here to get my money, and I intend to do just that."

I asked him, "Would you loosen the ties around my wrist? My fingertips are beginning to tingle a little."

Kenny yelled over, "Stop your yapping, woman. If anything, we'll tie them tighter."

Meanwhile Dillon had gone to get assistance. I knew the only people he would be able to get help from were his brothers. Knowing Dillon, he did not want to do that, but he did. Dillon told them what happened.

And oh boy, they were furious with him. Rusty was so angry at him that he slammed a chair against the wall. He turned red and began to shake and tremble at what Dillon had told him.

"How could you, Dillon? You nigger-loving animal! I knew we couldn't trust you. Now you think we gonna help you. Nooo way. For all I care, they can shred her to pieces."

Clyde was agreeing with the same sentiment. "Where is Floyd? He should be back by now."

Rusty replied, "I don't know, but I'm not helping Dillon with that old girl."

Clyde said, "Wait a minute, Rusty. I think Floyd went out that way walking, checking out the land."

Rusty asked, "Why don't we just call the police?"

Dillon wasn't listening to them. His mind was on Ruby. They had turned him down, so all he could do was think of another way to save her.

Rusty was looking at Dillon. "Dillon, do you hear me? We'll just call the police."

Dillon said, "Come on, Rusty, with all that marijuana you've got planted out there, no way we will not all go to jail. Now most likely they have Floyd and Ruby! Well, if you two won't help me, then I will have to go by myself."

Rusty and Clyde were looking puzzled while Dillon was preparing to go. They were looking at one another hesitating, but they saw that Dillon was serious and meant business, so they grabbed their guns, hopped in the truck with Dillon, and sped away like they were on fire. All anyone could see was a pillar of dust behind the truck.

Rusty said, "All I'm concerned about is Floyd."

While driving along, they began looking for the shack where Dillon had left me. When they got near it, Dillon said, "Stop here. This is where I left Ruby."

Once he entered the shack, of course I was long gone. Dillon became frantic, knowing that meant they had me. He grabbed a board leaning against the wall and threw it across the room. That was when he saw the opening in the wall. The boards were so loose that he began snatching them from the wall. He could then get in enough to see there was an opening into a tunnel.

He yelled, "Come on! There's a tunnel that leads somewhere."

They followed Dillon through the tunnel to the outside. Dillon said, "This must be what Ruby did. She heard them coming and came through here."

They began looking for some evidence that I had come through the tunnel once they were out.

Roscoe said, "There's got to be some tracks or something near."

They continued walking a long path, looking for clues. Then they came upon a dirt path. That was when the shoe prints began to show up.

"Look here," said Dillon in an excitement. "The tracks start here small like a woman's shoe, and there's a larger shoe print as well, which may be Floyd."

"You think they could have met up way out here?" said Rusty with a frown on his face from the hot sun.

Clyde replied, "Just don't make sense to me. Just don't make sense." But they all continued to look.

Floyd and I were still at the camp with the goons. I remembered there was a woman with them. *Where did she go, and why did she leave?* I never saw her face, and that seemed a little strange.

Kenny, the leader, told me to stop squirming so much, saying that it would be over soon. He told one of the other men, Scottie, to loosen the ties on my hands.

It was getting late in the afternoon, and Dillon had not found us yet. I was beginning to worry. The air was getting cooler. I was so glad that the other man, Sam, started a fire, which felt so good. Even through all the chaos that was happening, I closed my eyes and tried to think good thoughts to evade the reality of what was transpiring.

Kenny was the leader, and he led with an iron fist. The other two listened to him very well. They never disobeyed him. Scottie was short with brown hair and brown eyes. He had a stocky build and mustache. Sam was the slender one with thin brown hair and green eyes. They were all Caucasian men, but Scottie and Sam were followers so much that it seemed as though they were afraid of Kenny.

After Scottie had loosened the ties on my wrist, I could move my hands a little easier. It felt good to feel the blood flowing to my hands again. I tried to make myself as comfortable as possible since we were there for the night.

The afternoon grew cooler and cooler, but Sam continued to put wood on the fire. Although we had a nice fire going, it did not keep the animals away because we could hear their echoes in the dark. I heard the hooing of the owls and something walking in the nearby woods with leaves crackling on the ground. Maybe a racoon or bear. Who knew because it was so dark? At that point, I knew Dillon didn't know where to find me. The thought crossed my mind, *Did they even know Floyd was with me?* I was sure they would figure it out.

Kenny began to get impatient. "Where's that man of yours? You sure he's not sweet on somebody else because if he doesn't come on, there's gonna be two more bodies out here in these woods."

I told him, "Yeah, he's coming, but it won't be like you think. You see, he knows this area very well. He could be watching you right now as we speak."

They all grabbed their guns frantically, looking around. Floyd motioned for me to keep quiet by winking his eye. Floyd knew his brothers could be close by, and he didn't want me to spoil it. So I calmed down.

Meanwhile Dillon and his brothers did decide to stop looking because it had gotten dark, but they didn't give up. They slept in the truck until daylight. When the sun came up, they started again. Rusty started also.

The first thing he said was, "All of this because of that old gal." Then looking over at Dillon, he asked, "Is she really worth all this to you, Dillon?"

Dillon didn't even reply. He was so busy searching.

Rusty continued complaining. "We don't even know if they are dead or alive by now. Dillon, you went all the way back to New York City to get her. Couldn't you just let well enough do?"

"No, Rusty, I couldn't let well enough do. I love Ruby, and yea, she's worth it and more. I just hope some day, Rusty, you will find someone special too."

That was when Clyde butted in. "Yeah, and at least let's hope she is the same color as us."

Dillon explained to Clyde that he had discovered that true love has no color or boundaries. "It is pure without stipulations or conditions. It's being free to be me with that person and wanting to share all of my joy, hope, and dreams with them throughout eternity."

Clyde laughed. "That's a bunch of hogwash, and you know it." Then he spit on the ground.

"Well," said Dillon, "it may be to you, but it's real to me. Now come on. Let's look a little harder and stop complaining."

Dillon began to wonder why the mob would be out in this part of the country. He even questioned his brothers about it and why they would bring someone that far to kill them.

Clyde said, "I don't know, but what I do know is that this is a good place to get rid of a body, especially somebody you hate like that old Ruby. This just gives me an idea. Look at all these trees we have access to. We could hang old Ruby out here, and nobody would ever find her."

Dillon shouted, "Shut up! Shut up! Both of you. Is that all you can think about? How much you hate Ruby? Can you think of anything that she has personally done to you? What if she were a white woman?"

They looked at Dillon with a quick glimpse and turned the conversation to something else.

Dillon said, "Okay then."

Through all the madness that was going on, Floyd and I tried to remain as calm as possible. Sam had loosened the ties on my wrist, and I was able to maneuver my hands more through the ties, but I had to do it slowly so they wouldn't notice what I was doing. They were beginning to get sleepy. Kenny told Sam to stand watch while he got some shut-eye. That was when I realized there may be a chance to escape.

As Kenny snuggled down to take a nap with his cap over his face and legs stretched out, I noticed he was out like a light. He began to snore. Sam did like Kenny asked. He stood watch with his gun in his hand. Sam began to walk around the perimeter of where we were. The more he walked, the more I wiggled my hands to get free, and finally I did. I nudged Floyd, who was bobbing his head up and down.

I showed him my hands, and of course he was surprised. Meanwhile Sam had gone a little further out to relieve himself. That was when I untied Floyd's hands, and we both quietly began to move away from the camp quietly and slowly.

We barely had gotten ten feet away, and Sam came right behind us with his gun pointed at Floyd and me. He didn't even yell or seem to get excited. He spoke in a calm voice, as if he had done this a million times.

Kenny and Scottie heard what was going on and immediately hopped up. I caught them trying to escape.

"I believe it was the girl who got loose first, and then she untied the big fellow. You know, this is about to be more trouble than it's worth," said Sam.

Scottie added, "Yeah, Kenny, that old boyfriend of hers might have gone to the police."

Kenny replied, "No, I told you. We are miles from any police, and they don't have cell phones."

"Have you thought about a landline," asked Sam. "You know, Kenny, people still have those too."

"No actually I didn't, but did you see all that marijuana planted down in these woods as we were walking along?"

Kenny said, "I don't think they would want the cops to see all that now, would they?"

"How do we even know it's theirs?"

He then hit Floyd on head, yelling in his ear, "Come on, boy. Speak up! Did you and your brother plant all these plants down here?"

Floyd nodded his head yes.

"Now what did I tell you? I know these hillbilly types. They are not so friendly with the police. So we will take our chances. We have to stay focused."

Kenny ordered Scottie to make us sit down on the ground, tie our hands, and wrap a cord around the tree with us pinned against it, which was very uncomfortable.

It was daylight now, and there was no sign of Dillon. I was so tired of sitting on the ground. I asked Kenny, "Could we at least stand up on our feet for just a little while?"

He came over, loosened the cord, and yanked me up as hard as he could. I almost hated that I had asked him.

Floyd yelled, "Hey! Do you have to be so rough with her, man? You know she is a lady!"

Then Kenny said just for that statement, "You continue to sit there until your legs break." He then looked over at us. "Don't you two worry. You will soon be out of your misery as soon as that boyfriend shows up."

No sooner than he said that, an animal of some sort was making a noise in the leaves nearby. Scottie started shooting all at once into the area he heard the noise. He was so frightened by the noise that he was shaking all over.

Floyd began to laugh. "Y'all ain't used to the wild. I can see that." Then he laughed some more. It was so good to him that he continued to laugh.

Scottie said, "Shut up or I will bust you over the head! I mean it. Shut up!"

So Floyd quieted down, seeing that Scottie meant business. Floyd said, "I will tell you this though. If you shoot at every sound you hear out here, you will run out of ammunition fast."

I could see that it really appealed to Floyd, knowing they were out of their league out in the wild. Floyd knew he had the upper hand in that respect, looking at me and winking his right eye.

After Scottie's round of shots, I was hoping maybe Dillon or anyone who could help us heard them, but not a chance because we were deep in those woods. No one could hear us for miles. I looked across the green meadow. It was so beautiful, the way the sun shined down through the trees as if there were several spotlights shining through.

The moist dew on the grass glistened with the mist of tiny drops of water. Oh, how at that moment I would have loved to be a piece of grass blowing in the wind. Looking at the beautiful scenery in all its perfection gave me a sense of peace. It was almost as if it were a sign that everything was going to be all right, even though we were held captive against our will. I supposed I was still feeling sorry for myself. I began to sob with an ominous cry.

Floyd looked over at me. "Come on, Ruby. Hang in there. You've been my rock, so stay strong. I know you can do it."

He was encouraging me at a time that I really needed it. He even reminded me of one of my favorite scriptures from Psalm 27:3, "Though an host should encamp against me. My heart will not fear. Though war should rise against me, in this will I be confident." That scripture reminded me of a poem also that I had written for a friend. The title of the poem was "Be Strong."

They thought they had you binded and cornered.

They called you names and played games.

They even had you dishonored, yet you stood strong, knowing that in his arms you would prevail with no avail.

So go on marching strong, my friend. The end is not yet.

There's more to be met. Be strong, my friend. Be strong.

After remembering the scripture and poem, I began to calm down, feeling the strength within.

The three men gathered into a huddle and began to whisper among themselves. Floyd and I looked at each other. We were trying to hear what they were saying, but we couldn't. They kept looking back and forth at Floyd and me. The thought crossed my mind that maybe they had decided to get rid of us here and now. But Kenny did say he wanted us all together because Dillon had seen them as well.

Kenny turned to us and asked Floyd, "Do you know how to hunt for meat because everybody is getting hungry?"

Floyd replied, "Of course, but how am I supposed to hunt with my hands tied and no gun?"

Scottie said, "Shut up, hillbilly. Do you think I am stupid enough to give you a gun?"

Kenny said, "On second thought, let's not go through with that idea."

They made Floyd sit down on the ground. Kenny started looking around in the bushes. There were plenty of animals crawling through these woods. We should be able to catch something from nearby. As soon as Kenny said that, a wild turkey appeared out of nowhere.

Kenny chuckled. "Well, well, looka here."

He aimed to shoot the turkey and missed. The turkey darted behind some shrubbery and got away. He shot into the air several times out of anger and hunger, cursing with all types of obscenities.

Dillon and his brothers heard the shots ring out and ran back to the truck, heading into the direction of the shots. The old truck was rickety-rackety, but they sped off as fast as they could, making dust fly in the air like a pillar of smoke behind the truck. Once they got near the sound, they began to argue as to which direction it came from.

Dillon said, "I believe it came from that way."

Rusty replied, "Naw, it came from over there."

Clyde started yelling, "Shut up! Shut up! Will you make up your minds?"

They decided to go with Dillon's directions. As they got closer to the area, Dillon stopped the truck so the men wouldn't hear them coming. Dillon and his brothers got out of the truck, all dressed in their camouflage attire. As they walked closer, they could hear voices. Dillon motioned for his brothers to split up to surround the camp. Dillon threw a piece of wood out in the distance away from the camp.

Kenny jumped up and told Sam to go check it out. Sam went out and did not return because Clyde had hit him over the head and gagged him.

Kenny called out to Sam, "Sam, come on back!"

Sam didn't answer.

Kenny yelled, "Sam, cut it out. Come on back here now!"

Sam still didn't respond to the call. Kenny sent Scottie to get him, and Scottie didn't return. Kenny was looking frantic now, not knowing what to do. He began to turn from side to side with the gun pointed at anything that was to pop out of those woods.

I said, "Things are looking a bit strange around here. Wouldn't you say, Kenny?"

He looked at me with a grimace on his face and yelled, "Shut up! Let me think!" He began to sweat and roll his fingers back and forth on the gun as he held it. "Who's out there? Come on out, Sam! Scottie, come on out! The game's over now. Stop playing around."

Dillon stepped out of woods behind Kenny and told Kenny to drop it. That was when Rusty and Clyde came out also.

Floyd said, "Whew! Man, I thought y'all would never get here. What took you so long?"

When I saw Dillon, I ran and held on to him with all my might. He was looking me over, making sure I was all right. Even though Clyde and Rusty hated me, I was even glad to see them. They brought Sam and Scottie out of the woods, also with their hands tied and mouths gagged. Sam and Scottie had bruises on their faces where the brothers had hit them to keep them quiet.

The first thing Floyd wanted to know was where we could get something to eat.

Dillon said, "I think there's an old plank house not far from here. I don't know who lives there, but we can definitely check it out."

Finally we arrived at the house, a plain, small, wooden plank house tucked away in the forest with a pretty front yard, cut green grass, and a few flowers planted here and there. The house had a front porch with a railing built around it. It was a cozy, little country house.

Dillon knocked on the door, and Henry came to the door. He opened the screen door and was stunned to see us standing on his front porch. I was glad it was Henry. Although we didn't know each other that well, at least we had met before.

With a puzzled look on his face, he said, "Boy, what in de wul y'all done got yourselves into? What you holding guns on them boys for?"

Dillon replied, "It's a long story, Henry. I'll explain it to you later. Right now we are starving. Do you have anything to eat?"

"Yea, come on in." Henry yelled to his wife Lula to come over.

She came in, also stunned to see us standing in her house with guns. Lula moved a little closer to Henry with a frightened look on her face, asking Henry at the same time, "What's going on?"

He told her in a calm voice, "It's all right. I know these boys. They just want something to eat."

She began to calm down a little. Lula was a brown-skinned, elderly woman like Henry with a scarf wrapped around her head, African style. She was dressed very neatly with a denim skirt and a white blouse. She began to look in the cabinets and refrigerator for food. She found sandwich meat and bread. I asked her if I could use her bathroom to freshen up.

She said, "Yes, honey. It's down the hall on the right."

As I was walking down the hall, I saw pictures of her family on the wall. I could see they had a good life, a happy one. There were pictures of their wedding, parties they had attended, backyard barbeques, and some of their travels to other places.

When I came from the bathroom, I noticed Dillon had untied their hands to eat. I thought, *Oh boy! What is Kenny and his goons going to try next with their hands untied?*

I whispered to Dillon, "Do you think that was a wise thing to do?"

Dillon said, "Well, they gotta use their hands to eat with, and besides I got what I need right here in my hands." He pointed at his gun. "If they want to start anything."

My mind went back to some of the teachings I had learned while growing up in the church. We were taught that if you live by the sword, you die by the sword, not quoting it exactly from Matthew 26:52, but that was what it meant. I was not about to quote scripture to Dillon at that moment because I knew nothing was about to separate him from that gun. He held it with a passion for our protection, although I knew who the protector really was.

Mrs. Lula called Dillon to the side, and I could hear her telling him the exact same thing I was thinking. She said, "I don't know you, son, and you don't know me, but I see something in you not like them others. You ever hear, 'You live by the sword; you die by the sword'? All that means is violence begets violence, and if you trust in that weapon in your hand, it will only lead to more violence."

Dillon replied, "Yes, ma'am, I hear you, but I'm not at that level yet. I don't even go to church. I never have. I guess that's some of that spiritual stuff, huh? All I know, Mrs. Lula, is that I have to do what I have to right now, but thanks for the advice."

Mrs. Lula said, "Trust in the Lord, son. Just trust in Him, and He will see you through."

Everyone had eaten, so Rusty tied their hands again behind their backs while Dillon and Clyde held them at gunpoint. Dillon thanked Henry and his wife for the food.

Henry said, "I don't know what's going on, but looks like to me you could just call the sheriff. There's something else about them boys. It's like some kind of evil spirit other than what you see. You see, boy, I been around for a long time, and they carrying something other than guns."

Dillon replied, "No, we have our reasons for not calling the sheriff, and whatever else they are carrying, I believe we are ready for that too."

Henry looked at Dillon, smiling. "No, son, you're not ready for that."

Dillon didn't pay close attention to what Henry was saying at the moment. He thanked Henry and Mrs. Lula again. We started out on this long path.

Before we could get started, Dillon asked, "Kenny, why did you shoot the fellow back in the woods?"

Kenny answered with a cold look on his face, "He stole something from me, and I didn't get it back."

Dillon asked, "Like what?"

Kenny replied, "five million dollars. You don't just lose that kind of money and not know where it is."

"So it's out here?" inquired Dillon.

"Yeah, can you believe it, out here in no man's land? He said he couldn't remember where he hid it. He called the name of the place the Ox Bow, but he couldn't find it, so he said. In the kind of business we're in, you have to pay up or pay the cost."

Dillon replied, "You mean you outright killed that man because he didn't know where he hid the money?"

"You bet we did. How did we know whether he was telling the truth or not?" Kenny was jerking his shoulders around as if he were proud of what he did. "You can't take chances, man. What was I supposed to do? Let him go and let him come back to get the money, never to be seen again. No way was I about to let that happen."

Dillon already knew that would be Kenny's obvious response. That was why he stayed right with him, holding the gun on him.

We arrived back at the truck, and Dillon put the three men in the bed along with Rusty, continuing to hold the gun on them. Dillon told Rusty and the other brothers that they needed to go back and get that body just in case the police came down there looking around for him. "We don't want them to see all that marijuana planted down here."

Clyde said, "You know they won't come down here looking for that dead man 'cause don't nobody know he's down here."

Dillon added, "Well, maybe it's just my conscience. I can't leave a human being just lying out here. He at least needs a proper burial."

Rusty stated, "You mean you want us to ride back here with a dead body? Naw! No way. Ain't no way, Dillon! You can forget it."

Clyde said, "Maybe we could call Roscoe and Jasper. Maybe they could help us figure out this mess."

I looked at Dillon with my eyes wide open and mouth dropped, thinking, *No way! After all we've been through with those goons, how could Dillon even think of calling them?*

Kenny looked surprised, thinking that they didn't have cell phones.

Dillon said, "Remember—we can't get any reception out here, Clyde."

He was still focused on my expression as well. He then pulled me to the side to explain, "Roscoe and Jasper are also sheriff deputies."

I couldn't believe what I was hearing. "How could that be? Remember—these were the men who jumped on you at the dance for bringing me. They are not your friends. How can they uphold the law while going around beating up people for the color of their skin? Who put a badge in their hands to uphold the law? Just who?" I was getting angrier and angrier by the minute just thinking of it. My mouth began to quiver.

"Ruby, things are not always as they appear." Dillon had that serious, stern look on his face, which came naturally for him. It was the look that he had made up his mind and that nothing and no one was going to stand in his way. "Just because they have badges doesn't mean they are perfect. Okay, they're racist." He asked in a whispering voice, "Do you know how many police offers are walking around with hate in their minds and heart, whether black, white, Hispanic, or whatever color?"

Who would have ever thought that the two guys who jumped on Dillon at the dance were cops and the same two who participated in a car race? And actually they called the race.

Dillon said, "This is not the time for this argument. We have to get this body and these men out of these woods. Now come on!"

We drove back to where the body was. Rusty and Clyde put the body in the back of the pickup truck with the other men. Clyde looked at the dead man and said with a puzzled look on his face, "Umm, this guy looks familiar."

The other men in the truck looked at each other, wandering what he meant. We had gotten out in an area where Dillon thought maybe he could pick up some reception on his cell phone. So he called Jasper and Roscoe. But neither one answered. And by now, the body in the truck began to smell.

Sam said, "Look, you got to do something with this body. It's beginning to smell awfully bad."

Floyd yelled back at him, "Shut up! Just shut your trap! You don't have the right to say nothing. You should be lying there beside him!"

I noticed Scottie was being unusually quiet, not saying a word. He was staring at the body lying in the truck. He yelled out, "There's something in his shirt!"

Rusty pulled out his big hunting knife, slid it under the buttons of the shirt, ripped the shirt open, and saw a black snake. The snake crawled toward Scottie.

He yelled, "Oh, hell naw!"

The men in the truck had their hands tied behind their backs, but they managed to hop off the bed of the truck in fear. Rusty laughed, and oh boy, did he laugh at how frightened they were. He said, "Now here we have these big-time mobsters, and look-a-here, they scared of a little old black snake. Man, when we were kids, we would play with these things all day long."

Dillon added, "Okay, enough, Rusty. Let's get going."

Dillon tried to reach Roscoe and Jasper again on the phone. Finally he got a signal. Dillon explained what was going on. Jasper told Dillon that he and Roscoe would be there soon.

I asked Dillon, "How are you going to explain all the marijuana plants that were planted everywhere?"

"You don't think they know about that? Sure, you're right they are not my friends, but have you ever heard always keep your enemies close? And don't think for a moment that they don't smoke this stuff. They get it free from Rusty and Clyde all the time." Dillon spoke of it as though it was just a common, ordinary thing to do.

My mind was just boggled at that moment. All I could think of was, *Oh my God! Not only am I down here with hillbillies, a mob, and the lawless law, what next, Lord? What next?*

Kenny had a suggestion, seeing that Dillon and his brothers were in charge now. "Why don't you guys join us and help us look for the money? We will split it among us. You just untie us, and we'll all start searching for it. We find this place called the Ox Bow or whatever it's called and go from there. No one will have to know about the dead guy or any of this. We will bury him out here."

Of course, it looked as though Clyde and Rusty were all for it. They were scratching their heads with a puzzled look on their faces.

Dillon said, "Come on, you two. Get a hold of yourselves. Let's not get carried away about money. Remember—we're dealing with criminals here. Do you think for one second that they're gonna split anything with us? Think again. They will kill all of us first."

Kenny grinned a sly smile. "Just think about it, Dillon. Five million dollars. You know you could use it. You and your pretty little lady."

I was so glad when Dillon said, "No way. That's blood money, and I want no part of it. I may be a hillbilly to you, but I'm definitely not a stupid one."

Kenny, with an evil, sly grin, said, "Money is money."

Clyde was getting impatient waiting for Jasper and Roscoe. "I can't take the smell of this body anymore. Dillon, don't you have an old blanket or something in the truck to wrap this guy up?"

Dillon began looking around for the blanket. When he found it, he threw it over to Clyde to wrap the body. Clyde rolled the body over to wrap in the blanket. As he was lifting him over to place in the blanket, I noticed a mark on his side, like a birthmark. I couldn't help but notice the location and the shape of the mark. So I thought no more of it, but I knew I had seen it somewhere before.

Dillon also began to question the whereabouts of Jasper and Roscoe. "They should have been here by now. Jasper and Roscoe know this area just as well as we do. They can't be lost."

Dillon and I were still filthy from the swamp. All I wanted to do was sink in a nice hot tub and wash away all the stink, the tension, hostility, and chaos. I kept thinking, *If only we had not seen them kill that man, Dillon and I could be somewhere relaxing and enjoying this beautiful country.*

The mark on the dead man would not leave my mind. I pondered over it again and again. Then it came to me. I knew where I had seen it. I asked Dillon, "Hold up his shirt."

"Why?" But he pulled it up anyway. And there it was, the same mark on the same side as the dead man. "Why did you want me to pull up his shirt? What's going on?"

I explained, "The dead man has the same mark on his side as well."

He was so caught up with everything going on that he just shrugged it off. "That don't mean nothing. A lot of people have marks on the same spot. It's just a coincidence." And in the same breath, he said, "These guys better come on. We don't have all day."

We continued standing around, waiting for Jasper and Roscoe. Floyd decided to walk into the wooded area. He said it was to take a leak. He stayed for a few moments, and when he came out, there was Jasper and Roscoe. And who would have ever thought was with them? Naomi.

Jasper had his arm around Floyd's neck like a chokehold and a gun pointed to his head. Roscoe and Naomi also had their guns pointed at Dillon and his brothers and demanded that they drop their weapons.

Floyd said, "I think you better do as they say, guys."

Kenny moved close to Naomi. "Wow, babe. I thought you would never get back. What took you so long, and who are these guys? Come on and untie me."

We were all outraged at Naomi. She looked at Rusty. "Shut your mouth, Rusty, before you catch a fly."

When he did speak, he began to stutter with disappointment in his voice. As bad and mean as Rusty could be, I felt sorry for him at that moment. He and Naomi were close, brother and sister. They were closer than the others. We could almost feel the betrayal coming from Rusty as he spoke.

Rusty asked Naomi, "How could you take sides with strangers, especially people in organized crime? What's come over you, Naomi? Are you on some type of drug or under a spell? You weren't just my sister. You were my best friend."

Naomi looked at Rusty with a cold, cunning look and a sneaky grin on her face. "Well, let's just say, Rusty, when it comes to money, there are no friends or family. Only money. That's what counts."

Kenny had gotten impatient. He told Naomi again to untie him.

Naomi said, "Well, Kenny, there's been a change of plans. You see, I know you and I had a good thing going on, but like I said, when it comes to money, um, what's that song by Tina Turner? What's love got to do with it? This ain't about love, Kenny. I've got to get mine while I can. So I told Roscoe and Jasper about our little deal down here. I figured: who would ever be suspicious of two deputies involved in any illegal activities?

Kenny told Naomi, "We don't need any help. I've been in this line of work for decades, and there was no need to bring the law into it."

Naomi answered, "I want everything to look as legitimate as possible. I do not want to be involved with the mob for the rest of my life."

Kenny told Naomi, "Once you're in, you never get out. That's just the way it works."

"Well," said Naomi, "this is one that's getting out, and you better believe it. So to answer your request to untie you, the answer is no. I will not untie you."

Kenny looked at her in a despicable way. "I had a feeling you couldn't be trusted. When you left us back there, I thought you just freaked out about the shooting, but you actually ran off to get these guys, two hillbilly deputies."

Dillon looked at me and I at him. I knew we were thinking the same thing, *How much more bizarre could this situation get?*

Naomi yelled out, "What are you two looking at? I know you're judging me, but do you think I care? Dillon, how long did you think I was going to work at that convenience store? Forever, huh? No way. I have been thinking for a long time about how to get out of that dump, so I met Kenny. He came to the store one day on his way to New York, passing through, driving a fancy car, and wearing nice clothes. We started making small talk. Then I asked what he did for a living. He said he was in business for himself. Then I jokingly said, 'Well, I would like to be in business with you.' He said, 'If you are serious, here's my business card. Give me a call when you're ready to start.'"

Dillon mumbled, "Yea right, the business of killing people."

Kenny yelled out, seeing that he and his guys were out, "Naomi, why can't we continue to work together since we know the business and your guys know the law? This would be perfect."

Naomi whispered to Roscoe and Jasper about it.

Roscoe said, "Naomi, it's only a trick. You've double-crossed them, so now all of a sudden, he wants to join in with us. There's got to be more to it. Do you think they're going to trust you now?"

"That's easy," said Naomi. "These guys don't care about trust. They're greedy, but they do have a point." She even asked, "Dillon, would you like to join in, especially with all the marijuana you have growing down there? We could all make money."

Dillon answered, "I would never trust you again after this, Naomi, and to work with you, how dare you even ask!" Dillon even turned up his nose while looking at her. "You have definitely crossed the line."

The tension got high between Naomi and Dillon. Dillon replied, "Here you are, holding guns on your brothers and me, and then you ask to work with you. Naomi, you know where you can go, and if I weren't tied up, I would."

Naomi jumped forward in Dillon's face. "What, Dillon? You would do what?" They were going at each other like tigers. She pointed her gun at Dillon. "Keep talking. I got something here to shut you up, and I don't mind using it."

Jasper jumped in between Naomi and Dillon. "Wait, wait, wait a minute, little lady. We have to keep a cool head. We're going to need them to help us find that money now. They can't help us if they're dead now, can they?"

Rusty, Clyde, and Floyd looked on to see what Naomi's next move was because they were ready to defend Dillon, although they had guns pointed at them.

Kenny, being the sly fox he was, agreed with Jasper, anything to save his hide and gain whatever necessary. So it looked like Jasper and Naomi had the upper hand. They agreed to Kenny's proposition. Naomi untied Kenny, Sam, and Scottie.

Dillon looked at me with a great disappointment as if it were the end for us, but I knew my God would intervene. Although it looked hopeless as if our lives were about to end at any time, I kept hope alive. This was a time that I had to reach into my soul or spirit and rely on nothing but the power of the Almighty because to hope is to believe for something that is not seen. But faith bringeth that hope into fruition, making it come alive. As the sun comes up and goes down, so is hope and faith all the day long. That was all I had to help us.

I began to pray within myself at that moment. *Father, You see what we're faced against, how the enemy is encamped around us and we are at Your mercy. Only You, Father, can deliver us from this evil, so I'm asking You by Your mighty power and in the name of your precious Son, Jesus, deliver us. Amen.*

Roscoe and Jasper decided to bury the dead body. They insisted that Rusty and Clyde dig a place. They made Dillon, Floyd, and me sit on the ground while they dug.

Dillon asked Kenny, "Who's the dead guy?"

Kenny laughed. "Well, it doesn't really matter much now, does it, seeing that he's dead? What do you care anyway?"

Dillon replied, "Well, it just seems to me that somebody may come looking for him. Have you thought about that?"

"Well, they definitely won't find him down here, will they?" Kenny grinned.

I noticed Rusty and Clyde were making eye contact as if they were up to something. All of a sudden, Rusty fell to the ground. "Aw, aw, something bit my ankle."

Without even thinking, Naomi, being a little compassionate for her brother, ran over to check on him, not realizing it was a trick. Rusty grabbed her gun as she bent down to check on his ankle. He then put his arm around her neck in a chokehold, holding the gun to her head.

With a squeaky voice because of the tight hold Rusty had on her, Naomi yelled, "Shoot him, Jasper!" I was noticing how she was nurturing and kind at one moment and vicious the next. What a complex woman she was. She yelled to Jasper again, "Shoot him!"

Jasper was a little nervous pointing the gun at them, hesitating with uncertainty. Rusty told them to throw down their weapons right now. All of a sudden, out of nowhere, Scottie came up behind Rusty and hit him on the back of the head with a huge tree limb, knocking the gun out of his hand while he fell to the ground.

Rusty was a big, robust man, so it only stunned him for a few seconds. He began to come around, rubbing his head as dirt and grass fell from his hair and beard, adding to his already scruffy appearance. He was an awful sight. Naomi grabbed her gun once more and rubbed her neck.

Kenny applauded Scottie with a big old happy face. "Nice work, my man. Nice work."

They all had guns now except for Dillon, Rusty, Clyde, Floyd, and me. Jasper insisted that they continue to dig the grave. They dug and dug. It seemed like forever. I was exhausted just watching them. Finally when they were done, Rusty and Clyde slid the body from the truck, and while they were carrying the body to the grave, the dead man's shirt blew up over his chest. And that was when Dillon noticed the mark on his side also.

He looked at me and I at him. I knew he saw the mark, but he said nothing, and so did I. Then they dropped his body in the open grave like a sack of potatoes with no remorse, just evil. I thought, *God only knows how many others they have done this to.*

The mob crew was a treacherous bunch. They apparently were eviler than Jasper and Roscoe. The same evil resided in Naomi as well for her to team up with them. This, to me, was truly a day of evil. It felt as though I was walking through a black forest with no light and no end. Although I knew that it was just a feeling, I now knew that if I were to continue to go through whatever was to come next, then my mind would have to be elevated to a higher level because natural thoughts are natural and spiritual is spiritual. Therefore if I were to be of benefit to my brothers or myself, then I had to trust in the God I served and be led by His Spirit.

All the while they were digging and burying the body, Sam was watching Dillon in a seductive way. At first I thought maybe it was my imagination, but it wasn't. He looked at Dillon as if he could eat him. He even had a bulge in his pants. Although Dillon didn't see him watching him, I did, and Sam saw me as he jumped with amazement. He was embarrassed that I had caught him. Little did he know that Dillon was as straight as straight could be.

I didn't think Roscoe and Jasper actually knew who they were dealing with, but I could feel and see the coldness in their eyes. They were like vipers, ready to strike anytime. Their conscience was seared and burned out. All they had in mind was to kill, steal, and destroy. I thought Dillon and his brothers were tough and mean, but they were no match to this.

After burying the dead man, Jasper and Roscoe made us stand up on our feet. So Kenny began questioning Dillon and his brothers about the place called the Ox Bow. He was determined to find that money, no matter what it took.

He jabbed Clyde in the stomach with the butt of his gun. "Come on, boys! I know you hillbillies know something. You know how I know you know something. Look at you. You look like something grew up out of the dirt and has been here forever. So come on! Don't everybody speak at the same time. What about you, Mr. Dillon? Spit it out! Oh …" He looked at me. "What was I thinking? You got yourself a pretty little lady here, don't you? Well, why don't she and I go off over there in the woods and have a little fun while you figure out where this place is?" Kenny grabbed me by the hand and pulled me toward the wooded area.

I felt a chill go down my spine, almost a numbness at just the thought of Kenny touching me. At the same time, he was looking at me with a smirk on his face of confidence. His arrogance was repulsive, and with all that, he smelled horrible of musk and sweat. I looked back at Dillon.

Finally he spoke, telling Kenny to get his dirty hands off me. "Don't you dare lay a hand on her."

"Well, well, now he speaks." Kenny was anxious to hear what Dillon had to say, so he leaned over, putting his ear close to Dillon.

Dillon was squirming with his hands tied behind him, wanting to get free to get to Kenny. "All right, we'll show you where it is. Just let her go." He could see the fear in my eyes when Kenny mentioned taking me in the woods.

I continued to just believe by faith and not allow fear to overwhelm me. The thought of having to be with Kenny sent chills down my spine. I almost had rather been shot first.

Dillon yelled again, "Now take your filthy hands off her, and I mean now!"

Kenny backed off. "Okay, okay. So let's go, and if this is a trick, then me and the missus will keep our little date."

So we all headed to the area called the Ox Bow, with Dillon in the lead and Kenny behind him with a gun pointed to his back.

"By the way," Kenny asked, "how far is this place?"

Dillon replied, "Oh, about a couple of miles."

I thought, *I know that's not that far, but out of all that has happened, I am totally exhausted.* Kenny would jab the gun into Dillon's back repeatedly, pushing him along the way. Finally I just dropped to the ground and told them I couldn't go any further.

Sam grabbed me by the arm. "Get up, girl. Come on. We don't have that much further to go now!"

I just sat there. I couldn't move anymore.

Floyd yelled, "Leave her alone. Let her at least get her breath!" He mumbled under his breath, "Old dummies." Floyd was once more on my side.

It felt so good to sit down. Dillon was watching it all so intensely. Everyone was tense, not knowing what the other was thinking or what each one may do. Kenny decided that we all needed a break.

While we all sat there on the ground, I noticed that Scottie always carried a backpack, and I wondered what was in it. As we sat there, he pulled out a book and began to read. I don't know what he was reading, but it was very interesting to him. When he got up to walk away, several of the books fell from his bag. I could see some of the titles, which included books on war, politics, and poetry. And there was one with a star and a circle around it and other symbols on the book as well that I had no idea of what they meant. My thoughts went to something else.

I was sitting beside Floyd on the ground. He asked me, "How does Dillon know about this place, the Ox Bow?"

"I have no idea."

"I've never heard of it either. Maybe he's trying to buy time."

Rusty and Clyde managed to get close to us and asked the same thing. Floyd and I told them that we had no idea either what Dillon was doing. I just wanted it all to be over.

Then all of a sudden, we heard noises in the woods, like leaves rustling and then the growl of animals. We looked around, and all we could see were the teeth of several hungry wolves. Kenny, Sam, and Scottie began shooting at them. It seemed as though the more they shot, the more they came out of the woods. The others ran back into the woods.

As they were shooting, Rusty and Clyde decided to make a run for it. Kenny shot Rusty in the leg, and Clyde immediately stopped running. His leg was not bleeding very badly. They managed to get him back to where we were all sitting, so I pulled off my belt and tied a tourniquet around his leg to slow the bleeding down. After assessing the wound, I noticed that it was only grazed.

I told him he would be fine. He looked at me with amazement that I was helping him even though he hated me, but that was not who I was. I thanked my Almighty God that I was mature and educated enough to know that hatred is just ignorance. Clyde looked on with amazement as well, knowing how they had treated me previously. I proceeded to stabilize the wound with the belt. Thank goodness the bullet didn't penetrate deeper into the flesh. It only grazed the thigh.

Kenny yelled, "What do you think you're doing? Are you fools? You're gonna take off running with your hands tied behind your backs, huh?" He laughed. "I knew you were dumb but not that dumb. I could have killed you, but I didn't. Let that be a warning."

Kenny, Sam, and Scottie were so proud of themselves, having the upper hand on us.

Naomi clapped her hands while walking toward us. "Umm, nothing like a little excitement, huh, Rusty? Wow, Rusty, look how that old gal's helping you. Well, I thought I'd seen it all. As much as you hate her, I'm surprised that you even let her near you."

"Shut up!" said Clyde. "Can't you see the man's hurt!"

"Well, well, don't tell me you're getting soft, Clyde."

"Naomi, just shut your trap, you hear!" yelled Clyde. "Do you think Rusty and me want to hear anything you have to say? You're supposed to be our sister. Look at what you went and done. You done turn your back on us, following after them city slickers or whatever they is."

Naomi turned in slow motion with the rifle slung to her side and stretched her eyes wide open with no smile or grin on her face, a look of contempt, disgust, and rage. She raised the gun to Clyde's face. "Don't you dare speak to me about turning my back on you!" Every vein in her neck was pronounced. She began to yell, catching everyone's attention. "I know what you and Rusty did!"

Clyde looked puzzled, scratching his beard.

Naomi said, "And don't give me that innocent, dumb look. What? You didn't think I would find out about the land? How you and Rusty split the land amongst yourselves and left me out? Yea, I was tired of the convenience store, but more than anything, I was bent on getting back at you, my supposed-to-be brothers for not including me. Why, Rusty? Why, Clyde? And most of all, Dillon, you're not even related, and they gave you part of the land."

Dillon spoke up. "Naomi, I thought you were included. I guess I just assumed you were."

Rusty said, "Naomi, all I've ever heard you say is how glad you will be when you can get out of these woods, and besides, you're a woman. What would a woman do with that much land anyway?"

"So wait a minute," said Naomi with that same look of disgust on her face. "Let me get this straight. Rusty, so now not only do you hate niggers, you hate women as well. So Rusty, you're saying because I am a woman, I wouldn't have enough sense to own property. That's what you're saying, ain't it? That's what you're saying, you bastard." Naomi went into Rusty, slapping and beating him all over the head and face with his hands tied behind his back.

He was fair game because Naomi worked him over all like she wanted to. Naomi beat Rusty until she got tired. When she finished with him, his face was red and all bruised up with scratches everywhere. No one would help Rusty or stop Naomi. I suppose part of me liked seeing old Rusty get beat up, but by his sister/friend, that was a little sad.

After Naomi had beaten Rusty, Jasper stepped forward, admitting he was the one who told Naomi about the land situation. "Rusty and Clyde came to the courthouse concerning some land. They seemed to be quiet about what they were doing, so I followed them and kind of stayed behind them, watching which way they went. They went into the register of deeds office. After they left, I asked the clerk what they were there for, and she said they were checking on their land. I said, 'Their land?' I couldn't believe these knuckleheads owned land, but they did.

"That's when I went to the convenience store to confront Naomi about it, and of course as she said, she knew nothing, which infuriated her. After that, she and I became close. She felt like she had no one at the time, even though she was with Kenny. She knew it was only a matter of time before she had to end the relationship."

Naomi looked at Jasper with a seductive grin on her face.

I asked Naomi, "Do you know which of the two men you really want because it seems as though each of them has something you want? Kenny has the fast money; Jasper has information or can get it at the spend of a dime. Is there anything genuine about you, or is it all fake?"

Jasper looked on earnestly with a puzzled look etched across his face, waiting for a reply from Naomi, and boy, did she give it back.

Naomi said, "I do what I have to do when, where, and to whom, when and where it is necessary. You got that, half-breed?"

"Yes, and that's what I figured." Naomi had showed her true colors. There was no doubt about it.

Jasper, her lover, was speechless.

Kenny said, "Shut up, all of you! And let's get back to business. We've got to get this money and get out of here because I'm tired of these woods, the flies, gnats, mosquitoes, and, most of all, the yakking."

He was angry inside and hurt by the things Naomi had said. He was trying hard to elude his feelings, but there was a sad look on his face now with anger and bitterness built up as well as hurt. Naomi had turned on him and his colleagues. The harsh reality was that Naomi wasn't anyone's friend. She was all for herself. Although it seemed as if Jasper didn't mind, it almost looked as if they were of the same mind.

Rusty got up on his feet with the help of Sam and Scottie. I wanted to walk alongside Dillon, but they wouldn't let me, fearing we may try something.

Dillon asked Kenny again, "Who was the man who was shot in the head?"

Kenny said, "He was a nobody who took money from us, and that's all you need to know, not unless you want to end up like him."

Now we had finally come to the Ox Bow, which was supposed to be where all the money that the dead man had taken from Kenny and his gang. It was a beautiful meadow with lush green Kentucky grass and flowers of all sorts, like coleus, lantana, and pentas, just to name a few. I could see why anyone would want to come there. The aroma of the flowers was so sweet with a slight breeze blowing in the air.

Dillon said, "Hold up! Wait a minute. Now that we are here, I'm not going any further until you tell me who the man was that you killed! And I mean it. Go ahead and shoot me if you want to, but that won't get you your money."

Kenny looked at Dillon with a stern, stubborn look on his face. "I don't know why you're so interested in a nobody. I told you. He took money from us and hid it down in these woods, and if you got to know his name, it was Juice. I never knew his real name. That's what a lot of us do. We use a street name rather than our real names. It's like a code on the streets. Now that you are satisfied, let's find my money." He pushed Dillon in the back.

Dillon looked at me and I at him. We continued to walk along as I watched Dillon. I could see something was bothering him. Dillon was thinking of the dead man and the scar on his side. He went into deep thought about his childhood, his mother, father, and all the things he could possibly remember. In all of his thoughts, he saw his mother in the exact area they were in now. She was smiling and reaching out to him.

Dillon was so deep in thought that he stumbled, losing his balance and almost falling to the ground.

I asked him, "Are you okay?"

"Yes." But it was an uncertain yes.

At that point I was thinking, *If only I could read minds.* Dillon started to speak in a whispering voice.

"What? What did you say?"

He was trying to speak as low as possible so the others would not hear him. He said, "I do remember this place."

Kenny stated, "Okay, this is the spot. Now where would it be?"

Dillon started rubbing his head out of frustration. "I barely remember. I was very young when my mother would bring me out here. I didn't even remember those words, Ox Bow, until you said it, but somehow I remembered how to get back here."

Oh boy, I knew it was time to start praying again because Dillon couldn't remember, and now not only did Kenny have his gun pointed at us, but so did Jasper, Scottie, Sam, and Roscoe. We were sitting ducks.

Kenny said, "Everybody start looking under rocks, limbs, or whatever. Get to it now! Rusty and Clyde, don't just stand there looking at me."

Floyd told him, "Well, we can't do anything with our hands tied, can we?"

After our hands were untied, Kenny yelled out, "And don't do anything stupid."

All the while we were looking, I was praying to myself, *Please, God, let us find this money.*

Dillon heard me, and he whispered, "Even if we find it, they're still going to kill us. And don't think they won't. We've got to come up with a plan."

46

I was looking at Dillon with a hysterical look on my face. "What kind of a plan?"

"I don't know. Let me think." We continued looking frantically.

Kenny looked over and noticed we were talking. "Shut up, you two!"

Jasper said, "It's got to be a special place that he would hide it. So, Dillon, what was so special about this place? Think hard 'cause your life depends on it."

Naomi came over behind me and yanked my hair, pulling my head back. "Come on, girl. Get away from Dillon so he can think. He can't do nothing with you all up under him."

Everyone was tired and frustrated. Kenny's patience had come to an end. He just couldn't take it anymore. "Dillon, get on your knees! Now!" Kenny was getting ready to shoot Dillon in the head like he did the other man.

I said, "Woah! Woah! Wait a minute! Can't you see he's tired? We're all tired. Let's just sit down and catch our breath."

Kenny spoke with his gun pointed at us. "Shut up. I don't take no orders from no woman." He then ordered all us to get on our knees.

We got on our knees, and at that point, I burst into tears and began to call on the Almighty God. "Lord, if I be Your servant, grant me and these who are with me a deliverance this day. Stretch forth Thou mighty hands of love and mercy that this evil that is beset upon us is cast away."

Kenny was yelling, "Be quiet, woman, with all that mumbo-jumbo. Nothing will save you now. I've had enough of all of you."

When he said that, Sam said, "Aww, you don't have what it takes, Kenny. It's time to stop playing with these people. Let's get this over with." He pointed his gun at Roscoe and Jasper, shooting them in the head and killing them.

I jumped, shaking all over from the horror that had just happened. Naomi was screaming hysterically. Everyone's emotions were high.

Naomi ran over to Sam, beating him in the chest as hard as she could. She was yelling, "Why? Why did you do that?"

Sam told her, "If you don't get off me, you're next. They were in the way, damn it!"

Naomi didn't have her gun on her at the time. She would have shot Sam at that moment if she had. Kenny ordered Clyde and Rusty to throw the bodies down in a deep ravine nearby. Naomi then just sat down on the ground near a tree with a blank stare on her face. She was perhaps in shock. She was so hurt and devastated. Apparently she cared a lot for Jasper. She was so cold and heartless toward me that I found it hard to comfort her because I had not come to grips with all the things she had done to me. I knew we were supposed to forgive and forget, but at that moment, I had nothing to say.

Kenny asked Sam, "Who told you to take over? And now we have three dead bodies down here."

Sam was out of control. His eyes were red, and he was sweating profusely. He told Rusty and Clyde to find all the rocks they could after untying their hands. He said they'd better not try anything. Meanwhile Naomi was still sitting by the tree with that same look on her face, lifeless. Rusty tried to talk to her, but she remained quiet and still.

Finally Rusty yelled at her, "Come on, Naomi. Snap out of it!"

But there was no response. Kenny was looking on, enjoying every minute of Naomi's loss. He then walked over to Naomi, laying down his gun because of the blank look on her face. He thought she had completely lost her mind. He began to ridicule her. "Well, well, for once we have a quiet Naomi." He put his face close to hers.

Naomi grabbed his gun and pointed it at his face with tears streaming down her cheeks. "This is all your fault."

Kenny was backing away from her with his eyes stretched wide open at astonishment of her quick response. Staring down at the barrel of the gun, he was speechless.

"You're the one that brought that murdering bastard with you. I told you he was nothing but trouble, and now it's your turn."

Before she could pull the trigger, Scottie shot her in the chest. Naomi lay there on the ground lifeless. Kenny started running toward Scottie as fast as he could, slamming him to the ground and beating him in the face.

"Why did you have to do that?"

Scottie finally got a word in, wiping the blood from around his mouth. "She was going to kill you. Man, couldn't you see that? That bitch had lost her mind. She had gone crazy."

Kenny had no response. I looked over at Rusty. He was digging his heels down in the dirt while he sat on the ground, wagging his head from side to side, crying like a baby. "Why? Why, God? She never hurt nobody." He let out a cry like never before. Then he looked up at Scottie. "I will get you for this if it is the last thing I do."

Things had gotten really bad. Three people were dead, and it looked as if it were not going to get any better. Kenny and Sam began to mumble among themselves. Sam ordered Clyde and Rusty to find as many rocks as they could. Dillon and I looked at each other, wondering what was about to take place.

Clyde and Floyd did question him as to what he wanted the rocks for. But he just told them, "Do it and do it now!"

They found the rocks and put them all in a pile. Sam began to place the rocks in a circle. After he made the circle, then he proceeded to make a star in the circle. After completing the design, they tied Clyde and Rusty's hands and looked at us sitting there on the ground.

Sam said, "I bet you'll know where the money is after this. I was hoping it wouldn't come to this, but it looks like we have no other choice."

Sam got into the middle of the star and lay down on his stomach while Kenny and Scottie kneeled down on the edge of the circle, particularly at the point of the star. They began to chant some strange noises. The louder they got, the more the ground rumbled under the circle. Snakes began to come up from the ground and crawl around us, making hissing noises, but they did not bite. It was like an illusion but so very real.

I shut my eyes, praying it would be over soon. The crackling of the flames was a little distraction, but as the flames went up, Sam continued to mumble, calling on his spirits. And as he mumbled, angry faces appeared out of the flames, like demons making screeching sounds. I had never seen anything like it. I had heard of demons and devils before but never actually saw it, and now I was seeing it firsthand.

Dillon and his brothers seemed to have no fear, but for me, it was a nightmare. Dillon looked at me, knowing what I was going through. "Remember your faith. It's only a scare tactic. Look at me, don't take your eyes off me, and don't move."

We endured that torture for at least five minutes. Then the chanting stopped, and the snakes disappeared.

Kenny got up. "Oh, thank you, Sam, for that. I hope it has jogged your memory a little more. Tell me one more time where the money is."

Dillon replied, "If Sam can do all of what he just did, then surely those spirits ought to be able to tell you where the money is."

Kenny jabbed Dillon in the stomach with his fist. "Do you want more of what you just got?"

Sam interrupted. "You know what? Kenny I could always use another sacrifice 'cause I haven't offered up one in a while. They don't know where the money is anyway, or so they say. Either way let's sacrifice the girl, burn her while they watch, and kill them afterward."

Once again, they untied Dillon and Floyd, this time ordering them to find wood and stack it up. I was numb out of fear. I had gone through and seen so much that my body felt ragged and torn. My clothes were torn from the branches and limbs in the woods. Dillon looked so weary, tired, and sad as he looked at me. I felt as though I was prayed out. Where would the words come from? I had none. We had fought and tried, and now we were at the end beaten. All hope was gone. It appeared as if God had given up on us.

We were in the darkest of darkest and the lowest of lows. They had me tied to a tree. My back itched from the bark on the tree. With all my energy gone from hunger and exhaustion, my body was limp. My hair was dirty, and I smelled awful. But it was not just me. We all did. We could have all bathed for a day and still needed a bath.

I was not prepared for the horror that was about to take place. Being burned alive was definitely an evil injustice. I would have rather been shot. At least it would be over quickly, but no, this was their way of punishing all of us for not knowing where the money was. And at the same time, Sam got his token (a sacrifice).

Dillon and Floyd had finished stacking the wood in a pile. Dillon looked at me with his head hung down with no words. He didn't need them. I could feel what he felt and what he wanted to say. I heard it in my heart.

Floyd looked on, sobbing. "I love you, Ruby."

Scottie and Sam laid me on the pile of wood. It hurt so bad, but at least I was facing the sky to see, even if there were no hope left. I could at least see the beautiful blue sky because it wasn't quite dark yet. I told Dillon I loved him and that I would be waiting for him in eternity. He looked at me, biting his lips with tears flowing down his cheeks like huge raindrops. He was on his knees with his hands tied behind his back. I knew there was nothing he could do to save me.

I lay on the pile of wood, waiting for Kenny to light it, and I began to pray once more, looking toward heaven. "Lord, I'm Your child, and You said You would never leave me or forsake me. I'm crying out to You one last time to help me, please. This body that I am in belongs to You. My life belongs to You, but You also said if You be for me, then You're more than the whole world against me. Show me now, my Father, if You be for me this day, and remember Dillon and my brothers."

Kenny yelled, "Shut up with that mumbo-jumbo. It's over for you, girl." He then threw the match on the wood, and flames surrounded me.

I looked up at the sky and could see the clouds roll back, and I heard a voice saying, "Lay still, my child. Lay still." The flames got bigger and bigger, but I felt no heat.

I heard Sam say, "She's not burning. Why isn't she burning? She's supposed to be screaming her head off by now."

Scottie said, "There's somebody else in the fire."

Kenny was looking on with amazement. "I know we only put one person on that wood, but there's a man walking around it." He looked at Sam. "Is this some of your voodoo magic, Sam, 'cause if it is, you need to stop. And I mean stop it right now!"

Sam was looking on astonished at what he was seeing and shaking his head at the same time. "No, man, this is none of my doing."

The clouds became dark, hiding the sun. It began to thunder and lightning. Out of the woods came white horses with the faces of men. They made a circle around us as they pranced. Kenny and his men began to shoot at them, but it was useless because we could see right through them.

The horses cried out with a loud voice. "We are the host from on high. Put down your weapons now for thou shalt not kill."

But they continued shooting and yelling obscenities. They refused to listen to the spirits, and the earth under them opened, consumed them, and immediately closed. There was not one trace left of them, as if they never existed. The dark clouds rolled back. The sun began to peek its light through the trees with a quietness of beauty.

I stood up on my feet from the pile of wood I laid on to acknowledge and thank God for what He had just done. Dillon and the others just sat there for a few seconds, looking at one another, shaking, and trembling.

Rusty said, "Somebody tell me what in the hell just happened."

I replied, "Rusty, you just witnessed a miracle from God."

He stepped back from me. "And you're the one who started it all with your mumbo-jumbo praying. Get away from me." He asked with a tremble in his voice, "What are you, some kind of witch?"

I knew how he felt, and I tried to console him, but he didn't understand.

He said, "God didn't have anything to do with this. Didn't you see, girl?" He screamed at the top of his voice, "What just happened here? God doesn't do stuff like that. Them people just disappeared in the ground." His eyes turned red and filled with tears, and he began to cry a little. The almighty Rusty crying, I couldn't believe it. They were all amazed and scared at the same time.

Dillon grabbed my hand and looked me over in amazement. "Wow, not even a hair on your head is burned, and who was that in the fire with you?"

"I saw no one. I only heard a voice saying lay still."

Dillon said, "Oh yeah, there was definitely somebody else there with you. We all saw it." He pulled me to him. "Woman, I didn't know you could pray like that. Who taught you how to do that?"

"It was neither taught to me nor read. It was by the Spirit of God. The Spirit knows all things, and when you pray with a sincereness from the heart, God hears and answers. Sometimes it's right then; other times it's later. And if it is not His will, maybe never."

Floyd asked, "What about the spirits we saw?"

"What about them?" inquired Dillon. "Floyd, why don't we just leave it as it is, spirits? We don't know, but like Ruby said, it's God's work. He does things like He wants to when and where. I'm learning too, Floyd, about the ways of God."

All the time we were talking, Clyde had his back turned to us. I went over and tapped him on the shoulder. He jumped and began to shake. He backed away.

"Get away from me. Don't touch me." His face was full of fear; his eyes were bulged out. He began to run as fast as he could through the woods.

Dillon took off after him. "Stop! Stop! Clyde!"

Finally he stopped running, and Dillon asked, "Come on, man. What's wrong?"

Clyde replied, "Didn't you see all that? Man, the world's coming to an end." His body was shaking all over; his hands were shaking. He looked up at the sky with a puzzled look on his face. "I-I-I never seen anything like it." Clyde broke down in tears. "Dillon, am I crazy or just losing my mind?" His tears streamed down his face. "All those people were just zapped down in the ground. Can't y'all see we need to get out of here before the same thing happens to us? Didn't you see those horses with the faces of men? I've never seen anything like it and don't want to ever again."

Dillon said, "Yeah, Clyde, but look at us. We're still here." Dillon was excited that we could hear it in his voice.

Clyde was looking around to see if anything else were about to take place. He began to calm down as Dillon continued to talk to him, and finally Dillon convinced him to come on back with us.

After all that had transpired, we looked around and saw debris lying on the ground all around us. All the beautiful flowers lay scattered across the ground. Limbs had fallen from the trees. Everything had been disturbed except one tree that stood in the middle of the Ox Bow, a red buckeye tree, which is native to Kentucky.

We all were amazed at the tree standing there alone. We walked over to it. There was also a rock leaning against it. Dillon pulled the rock back because it looked as though something was behind it, a black duffle bag.

Dillon opened the bag and saw a ton of money in it. "All this time, this is what they wanted. Well, I guess we'll have to turn it in to the police."

Rusty yelled out, "Man, have you lost your mind? How are you supposed to explain all this? So, Dillon, we are going to the police and tell them how we saw horses with faces like men and how Kenny, Scottie, and Sam were all just zapped down into the earth. It's just too bizarre, Dillon."

I couldn't believe there were actually tears streaming down his face. He was showing some humanity. Who would ever thought it was possible for Rusty or Clyde to show that side of themselves?

Rusty said, "I've never seen anything like that in my life, and I won't ever forget that as long as I live."

Meanwhile Dillon continued to dig into the bag. He found an envelope at the bottom. Dillon pulled it from the bag and said with amazement, "Wow, it has my name on it. This is so weird. Here's an envelope with my name on it."

Stunned, he just stood there looking at the envelope. We all gathered around to see what was in it. Finally Floyd said, "Come on, Dillon. Open it."

Dillon began to open the envelope slowly with a puzzled look on his face. There was a letter inside, of course. Dillon proceeded to read the letter out loud.

> Dillon, my brother, I know you don't remember me because we were so young when they separated us, but I never forgot you. I also know that if you are reading this letter, then I am no longer alive. I had such high hopes for us, Dillon, that we would reunite one day and do fun things together like fishing, hunting, and going to ballgames, things that brothers do, but apparently it wasn't meant to be. Funny, huh, how our mother would bring us down here to play quite often, and somehow you remembered this place, the Ox Bow. I also know you're wondering how I got mixed up with these guys. All I know is that I made a lot of bad choices in life and that's why I came back home, or should I say I wanted to come back home to start over. I read somewhere or either heard someone say, 'Trust in the Lord with all thine heart, and lean not unto thine own understanding. In all thy ways acknowledge him, and he shall direct thy paths' (Proverbs 3:5–10). Those words have stayed in my mind and heart for a long time. Although I never

lived it, as you can see, maybe if I had, I would have had a better and longer life. I never went to church and was never was a religious man, but I thought about it a million times. I know you're looking at all the money, and yes, I took it from Kenny and his gang, but of course, it's yours now to do with it whatever you want. Take care, my brother. You were always in my heart, and don't forget to let Him direct your paths.

Rusty, Clyde, and I were looking at Dillon at this point, waiting for his response. Dillon sat down on the ground in amazement, and at the same time, tears rolled down his cheeks.

"My one and only blood brother. They killed him like an animal with no remorse, no conscience, no shame. He was on his way back home." Dillon was sobbing with a great hurt in his heart. "I never got a chance to know him. I feel I've been robbed of something I never had."

Clyde, being the heartless man he was, told Dillon, "Snap out of it, man. Just look at all this money. We're rich."

Rusty, of course, agreed with Clyde while Floyd remained neutral.

Dillon stood up in anger and remorse. His voice was trembling; his hands were shaking. He told Rusty and Clyde, "Shut up! No one's taking this money anywhere. This is blood money. My brother was killed over this paper. It's just paper he died for. A bag of paper. Oh yeah! We could spend it, but at what expense? My brother lost his life slamming his hand into the tree. How many more out there have to die for this money? We don't know, do we? But my brother is just one that we know about. No, we are not taking this money anywhere. Matter of fact, let's burn it."

Dillon proceeded to take a lighter from his pocket to light the bag of money.

Rusty knocked his hand away. "Why do you get to make the decision, Dillon? Why don't we vote on it?"

Dillon said, "All in favor, raise your hand."

Only Clyde and Rusty raised their hands.

Rusty was so furious that he grabbed the bag. "Come on, Clyde. Dillon's a fool. Let's go."

Dillon grabbed the bag by the strap, and both were wrestling with the bag and falling to the ground. Dillon managed to get up while Rusty was still down. Dillon grabbed a huge rock nearby and raised it in the air to hit Rusty.

I immediately jumped in front of Dillon at that moment because he had the rock raised above his head to smash Rusty. "Stop! Dillon, please stop! Don't hurt him. He's your brother too. Maybe not in blood, but in life."

He dropped the rock and fell on his knees, thinking of what he almost did. "I can't believe what just happened. I was about to kill you, Rusty, all because of money."

Rusty said, "Yeah, man, we never went at each other like that before, so Dillon, you may be right. Let's burn it." So they did.

Rusty looked at me. "Ruby, you may have just saved my life."

Clyde said, "Yeah, man, I think she did. That was a huge rock."

Rusty was looking at me, shaking his head. "You mean after all we put you through, you still looked out for me."

I said, "Well, the good book tells us, 'Therefore all things whatsoever ye would that men should do to you: do ye even so to them' (Matthew 7:12). In other words, Rusty, it's the golden rule of life: do unto others as you would have them do unto you."

"Okay! Okay!" Rusty cringed. "Enough of that preaching. You really like that preaching stuff, don't you, Ruby?"

"Yeah, I do, Rusty. Matter of fact, I love it."

Clyde still wasn't in agreement with everyone about the money, but he was outnumbered.

When we returned home, we never spoke of what happened again down at the Ox Bow, and strange as it may seem, no one even questioned us about Naomi, Jasper, Roscoe, and the others, which was good on our behalf because it would have been very hard to explain. It was as if the memory of them was wiped away, never to be thought of again.

Dillon and I stayed at the brothers' house or, should I say, my brothers' house until we could get my car out of the ravine. The first thing I wanted was a hot shower. It felt so good to get a shower. The water streaming down felt as though all that had transpired was being washed away, but reality was there to confront me that it would definitely take time for all of us to heal from the trauma.

They were a little kinder to me this time around. Things were going quite smoothly, so that's when I decided to tell Dillon the wonderful news that we were going to have a baby. He was outside getting some things out of the truck.

I approached him, smiling. "Dillon, I have a surprise for you."

He stood up and looked at me. "Oh no! What is it now? Can't we just have a moment of peace around here?"

"Dillon, I am pregnant."

He looked at me. "You're kidding me, right? You've got to be kidding."

"No, I am not."

"Wait! It was only one time. Are you sure really? You mean I am going to be a dad?" He jumped in the air, yelling "hot damn," letting the country boy in him show with all he had. He then picked me up and swung me around. Then he quickly put me down. "Oh, I forgot. I have to be gentle."

He ran into the house, screaming to his brothers that he was going to be a father. His joy was ecstatic, but the look on his brothers' faces was anything but. Clyde had a contemptuous look written all over his face. Rusty had his mouth dropped open a mile long.

Clyde yelled out, "Shut up! Don't you realize what you're saying, man? I can't believe you're happy about a mud baby."

Dillon's joy quickly turned to anger. He balled up his fist and hit Clyde so hard that he knocked him across the floor without even thinking. He looked at Clyde on the floor. "Don't you ever refer to my child as a mud baby again as long as you live, you racist pig."

I didn't go after him. I thought it would be best that he cooled down a bit. Rusty straightened his face while clearing his voice and actually said while helping Clyde up on his feet, "That's good news, Ruby. Clyde will be all right." He looked at Clyde. "Ain't that right, Clyde?"

Clyde was rubbing his jaw and had nothing to say. It pained Dillon for Clyde to humiliate his unborn child. I could see the hurt in his eyes.

Dillon asked, "How could someone be so cruel to a human being who hasn't even entered the world yet? Clyde is just evil! Evil! Evil! There is no hope for him. I almost hate him."

"Whoa, whoa," I told him. "1 know you're upset, but don't use that word. That is a powerful word. It has horrible effects. It is the opposite of love. If you allow hate to enter in, then you are no better than Clyde. Hate will dive deep into your very soul and refuse to let go. Then comes anger, bitterness, wrath, and negativity, which breeds more hate because you will carry it everywhere you go." I begged him to please refrain from using that word.

He began to calm down. I had to remind Dillon that Clyde had a mental problem so deeply embedded that it would take God, prayer, and professional help in order to help Clyde. He moved close to me and hugged me.

"What would I do without you?" He began to rub my stomach with a proud look on his face.

I could feel he was very proud of the fact that he was going to be a dad.

Dillon and I discussed whether or not to tell them that we were going to get married since the news of the pregnancy had upset them so much.

Dillon said, "Well, we might as well do all our fighting in one day and get it over with." He looked at me smiling because he knew I was not having it.

We went back inside. Dillon then told them all that he had an announcement. "Yes, I know. Another surprise. Ruby and I are getting married soon because the baby can't wait for us to put it on hold."

Floyd yelled out, "Yes!"

Even Rusty said, "Congratulations, man."

Clyde said, "No comment."

Dillon said, "I know you said soon, but when and where?"

I spoke up. "I know of the perfect place."

Dillon looked down at me, smiling. "Just where would that be, my dear, looking ever so handsome?"

This was the exciting part for me, which was worth all that I had gone through. They stood, waiting with anticipation to see what I was going to say.

"You will have to travel a bit because it's located in Nashville, North Carolina."

Rusty said, "Hold on a minute. Now you expect us to travel to North Carolina." He scratched his beard with a puzzled look on his face. "Do you know that's asking a lot of us because all we know about is these Kentucky hills? We ain't never been outside of Kentucky."

Floyd added, "Come on, Rusty. It will be fun to go to a wedding."

I continued, "Yes, that's right, Floyd. It will be good for all of you to get out of Kentucky for a little while, and of course you will fly."

No sooner than I could get the words out of my mouth, Floyd was out the door, running like a streak of lighting. I ran behind him, trying to catch him, but for a heavy fellow, he was faster than I'd seen him before.

Finally I caught up with him. Both of us were out of breath. I asked him, "What's the problem?"

He was still trying to catch his breath. "Fly. You said we would have to fly. You see, Ruby, I could never see myself up in the sky in one of dem things 'cause, Ruby, when day fall, you dead. You hear me? You dead. It's no more Floyd."

"Okay! Okay!" I could see he was petrified of flying. Continuing to get my breath, I said, "All right, Floyd, I just thought you and your brothers might want to get there and back faster."

Floyd replied, "Come on, Ruby. Can't we just ride in a regular vehicle?"

"Of course you can. I will ask Dillon to rent a car. That sounds better, huh?"

Floyd said, "Oh yeah, I will definitely be there."

We went back inside with the others. They were all waiting to see what had happened to Floyd. Clyde thought it was so funny that Floyd had a fear of flying that he laughed hysterically.

Rusty was smiling. "Come on, Floyd. It can't be that bad."

Even though I hadn't done it either, I said, "Okay, may we continue about where the wedding will be? The place again is in Nashville, North Carolina. The wedding will take place at the

Rose Hill Plantation. It's a beautiful plantation house nestled down at the end of a long path out in the country with crepe myrtles on both sides of the path with rose bushes planted along here and there. And as you're driving along and look across the hills, there's black cows scattered on the hilltops.

"At the end of the path, you come to a huge, beautiful house sitting on a hill with huge, white columns at the front of a wide porch. There is a water fountain right in front of the house to set off its grandeur. The house is beautiful, but I prefer to get married outside on the grounds. There is a gazebo near a pond with lush green grass, which is a spectacular view."

Dillon stopped me. "Wait a minute. How do you know of this place?"

"I had gone there to another friend's wedding."

Dillon was looking confused for a moment. "Didn't you call this house a plantation house?"

"Yes, I did."

Dillon was still looking confused. "And you sure that's where you want to do get married, at a place like that, after all you've been through?"

"I hold no grudges. What happened to me is happening all over the world. Even at this very moment, someone is being discriminated against because of color, sex, nationality, and religion. What are we supposed to do? Just stop living because of the haters? Of course not. We rise to the occasion and confront it with wisdom that peace will abound and, most of all, prayer that God will intervene. We let the haters go on hating and the lovers go on loving because in the end, we all know love conquers all.

"It is a great feeling inside oneself to not have to hide the fears and anxieties of discrimination, which is that dark side of an individual that does not want to be revealed to everyone, only a certain sect. It is a momentous experience when an individual realizes that we are all created equal in the eyes of God, and that, my friends, is true freedom. Wouldn't you all agree? It's time for the past to meet the present." I pointed at my stomach and the future.

"Sounds good to me," said Dillon. "Let's do it."

My heart was glad. It was a joyous time. I packed the few things I had brought with me, said my good-byes, and headed back to New York. Dillon stayed home while I returned to New York to make wedding plans. I notified Katherine that once again I would be getting married, only this time to a different man and a different place.

She knew of the man, but she asked, "What place?"

"Nashville, North Carolina."

She couldn't believe it because she was also there when our other friend got married there as well. We were both excited.

While I was busy making plans with Katherine, Dillon was finding a home for us in Kentucky. My practice was doing great, and I didn't want to leave that part of my life behind, but I knew I could start over in Kentucky.

There were so many new beginnings in my life: a new baby, a new husband, and a new home. All of a sudden, I became overwhelmed and began to have panic attacks. I saw my doctor, and she said to slow down, especially being pregnant, and to get plenty of rest.

When I told Katherine, she was all over me like a mother hen. She told me that I had to move in with her until the wedding, which I didn't think was necessary. I didn't bother to argue about it, so I did. Katherine was an amazing friend. She was the sister I never had.

Katherine and I were sitting at the table having breakfast and coffee when we heard a knock at the door. Katherine ran to answer it. It was Bryan, my former fiancé. We greeted each other with a hug.

"I've been trying to call you but didn't get an answer, so I took a chance and came over. I also went over to your house and saw that no one was there. That was I got worried and came to Katherine's." Bryan stood back from me. "Look at you, girl. You look great. You have a certain glow about you. I guess that country air agrees with you, huh?"

I dared not tell him I was pregnant, knowing that our faith did not condone that type of thing, and on that note, Katherine excused herself from the room.

With a sarcastic grin on his face with both dimples imprinted, Bryan asked, "How's that old country bumpkin doing?"

I smiled back. "That old country bumpkin, as you put it, is about to be my husband."

"Oh yeah, how can I forget that indecent proposal? Ruby, do you realize how bad I wanted to punch that guy that day? It took every ounce of God in me to hold my peace. The nerve of that guy to just walk in and break up our wedding, but it was not meant to be. If it were, then we would have proceeded to be married, and as they say, may the best man win. He won, and that's why I am here, Ruby, to wish you the very best. I am just so happy to have had you in my life, and I hope we will always be friends, no matter what."

"Oh yes. Of course, let's not ever stop caring for one another."

We both agreed, and as he proceeded to leave, I asked, "Would you like to come to the wedding?"

"I don't know. I will have to think about it. In my heart, Ruby, you're still my girl, and I don't know at this point if I can bear the thought of seeing you marry someone else."

"I would love for you to be there despite all that has happened."

He just dropped his head without an answer. He smiled and walked away.

Katherine and I made of list of who and how many would be coming to the wedding. We already knew she would be my maid of honor. We chose five bridesmaids and five groomsmen. I decided to use a wedding planner this time because Katherine had worked so hard planning the first wedding, so I wanted her to just relax this time.

All of my friends and acquaintances were eager to go to North Carolina. Some had never gone there before, and they were excited to see the Rose Hill Manor. I knew it was not going to be easy for Dillon to get his brothers from Kentucky to North Carolina, even though we had discussed it, but still I kept hope alive.

I couldn't stop thinking about it, and I decided to call Dillon and inquire about how things were going for the trip.

Dillon said everything was going well. "Believe it or not, they even went out and bought real suits," said Dillon laughingly. "Could I drive my truck instead of renting a car?" He knew his truck was an eyesore.

"Do you still want to get married?"

He instantly said, "Of course! You know that."

"Okay then. That's your answer about the truck, funny man."

Three days before the wedding, we arrived in North Carolina at the Raleigh-Durham airport. We drove Rocky Mount, North Carolina, which was about fifty miles away, to find the nearest motel to Nashville. It was good to know that Nashville was only ten miles from Rocky Mount.

I called Dillon to see how far they had gotten. He said they were in North Carolina as well and it wouldn't be long. We could all meet at the motel together. The wedding planner called. She was anxiously waiting to get started with the rehearsal. Everything was coming together nicely.

On the day of the wedding, Dillon and I met to eat breakfast at the motel to have a little quiet time together. He told me that he had invited Henry and Lula to the wedding and that he wanted Henry to give me away. I was surprised and happy that he had even given it a thought. He said Henry was a good man, and I thought so too.

The quiet time didn't last long because all his brothers decided to join us at breakfast. It was fine. I was just glad to know they had wanted to come along and be a part of the wedding.

Floyd said, "We drove down to that Rose Hill place, and Ruby, you're not kidding. That is something to behold. I see why you want to get married there. It's amazing."

Rusty added, "The trip over here from Kentucky was pretty amazing too. Maybe I need to get out of Kentucky more often."

Clyde just sat, saying nothing for a moment, and then he spoke. "Well, it's all nice and all, but I'd still rather stay just where I am in Kentucky. That's where I was born, and that's where I'll die." He then grunted. "You won't be dragging me around the countryside and what fer, seeing stuff. I see enough right in Kentucky."

Dillon said, "Okay, Clyde, nobody is going to twist your arm to travel. Some of us like to go, and some of us don't.

After breakfast, I headed over to Rose Hill to start preparing for the wedding. The decorations for the wedding were beautiful with flowers and ribbons everywhere. There was even a white carpet rolled onto a boardwalk leading up to the gazebo.

My dress was white satin at the top and ball gown at the bottom. The wedding planner had someone there to help with putting the gown on, along with doing my makeup and hair. As the hairdresser fixed my hair, I was looking at myself in the mirror, thinking, *How did I get this far after all that has transpired over the last few months? How did one night on a dark, empty road turn my life around?*

That night was the beginning of my life. A wrong turn can sometimes be the right turn. I was so overwhelmed with love and joy in my heart at that moment that it felt as if I were to burst and there would be flowers and sunshine all over the floor.

It was now time for the wedding to begin. Everyone was gathered together. The ceremony had started. Dillon was standing at the altar waiting. Then I heard a knock at the door. It was Bryan.

He said, "I just wanted to see you for one last time. Ruby, you look amazing. That dress is even prettier than the other one." He even teared up a little. "I can't stay, but I did want to get just one last look at the one friend whom I held dear to my heart." He gave me a slight kiss on the cheek and left.

It was now my turn to walk down the aisle. The soundtrack was playing Ed Sheeran and Beyonce, the perfect duet. Henry was sitting in the back waiting for me. As I entered, he stood up and wrapped his arm around mine as we walked to the altar.

When we got there, he placed my hand in Dillon's. That was when the bridesmaids made their entrance doing an African Kenyan dance. I knew this was Katherine's idea because I was totally shocked. Katherine looked at me, winking and smiling. The bridesmaids were beautiful. They wore peach-colored gowns and had natural hairstyles, Afros, and braids.

When I thought that was all, then came the groomsmen with another type of dance. They were clogging with a little hip-hop move, which was awesome. They were dressed in black tuxedos. Katherine once again looked at me smiling.

We then proceeded with the vows. We didn't write our own. We decided to use the traditional ones. At the wedding reception, Katherine told me when she heard that I was going to marry Dillon, she started working on the dance routine for the bridesmaids and groomsmen. They even did another dance together at the reception. The bridesmaids and groomsmen performed together.

I looked behind them and saw Rusty, Clyde, and Floyd clogging as well. I punched Dillon, telling him to look.

Dillon said, "Oh yeah, that's the only dance they know and are good at too."

And actually they were. They were in step all the way.

It was a beautiful wedding. I enjoyed it. I think everyone did. Dillon and I said our good-byes to everyone and flew back to Kentucky to start our new lives together, waiting for our new arrival.

Printed in the United States
By Bookmasters